Best Fillies Forever

My Little Pony: We Like Spike! originally published in September 2015
by Little, Brown and Company

My Little Pony: We Are Family originally published in April 2017
by Little, Brown and Company

My Little Pony: The Gift of Maud Pie originally published in October 2016
by Little, Brown and Company

My Little Pony: Pinkie Pie Keeps a Secret originally published in April 2016
by Little, Brown and Company

My Little Pony: Meet Starlight Glimmer originally published in January 2017
by Little, Brown and Company

My Little Pony: We Are Unicorns! originally published in May 2018
by Little, Brown and Company

Cover design by Cassie Gonzales

Little, Brown and Company
Hachette Book Group
1290 Avenue of the Americas, New York, NY 10104
Visit us at LBYR.com
mylittlepony.com

First Bindup Edition: September 2019

Little, Brown and Company is a division of Hachette Book Group, Inc.
The Little, Brown name and logo are trademarks of Hachette Book Group, Inc.

The publisher is not responsible for websites (or their content)
that are not owned by the publisher.

ISBN: 978-0-316-48698-9

Printed in China

APS

10 9 8 7 6 5 4 3 2

Licensed By:

Best Fillies Forever

LITTLE, BROWN AND COMPANY

New York Boston

Contents

We Like Spike!

by **Jennifer Fox**

LITTLE, BROWN AND COMPANY
New York Boston

What is purple and green
and came from a tiny egg?

It is our friend Spike!

He is a Dragon.

He is a cute little guy.

He is a great friend
and a super assistant.

Spike uses his magic fire breath
to send scrolls.

He is always ready to help.

Spike works really hard.

He also knows how to have fun!

Spike likes to read comic books.

His favorite heroes

are the Power Ponies.

He likes to laugh and
can be very silly!

Our little Spike is
a total sweetheart.

22

He also has a big sweet tooth!

Spike bakes yummy gem cakes.

Most of the gems do not
end up in the cake!
They end up in his belly!

27

Spike is not a pony,
but he is family.

28

We like Spike!

We Are Family

My Little Pony

written by **Magnolia Belle**

L B

LITTLE, BROWN AND COMPANY
New York Boston

Attention, My Little Pony fans!
Look for these words when you read this book.
Can you spot them all?

Castle of Friendship

magic

bakery

sports teams

In Ponyville, family is as
important as friendship!

Twilight Sparkle is a
part of many families.

Twilight lives in the Castle of Friendship with Spike.
He is her best friend!

She also lives with her pet,
Owlowiscious.

Twilight loves Spike and Owlowiscious.
They are a family!

Twilight loves her parents, too.
She is great at magic because
her parents are Unicorns, too!

Twilight has a brother.
Shining Armor is married
to Princess Cadance.

They have a baby named Flurry Heart.
Twilight is Flurry Heart's aunt!

Flurry Heart is not the only baby
in Equestria.

Mr. and Mrs. Cake's twins are named
Pound Cake and Pumpkin Cake.

Fluttershy also has a brother.

His name is Zephyr Breeze.

Twilight and Fluttershy do not have
sisters, but Pinkie Pie has three!
They work with their parents.

Rarity also has a little sister.

She is very helpful.

Her name is Sweetie Belle.

Applejack has a brother and sister.

Big McIntosh and Apple Bloom

live with Granny Smith.

She takes good care of them.

Rainbow Dash does not have
a sister or brother.
She is an only child.
She looks out for Scootaloo
like a big sister.

Sometimes brothers and sisters fight
and hurt one another's feelings.
And sometimes they are the
best of friends.

Princess Celestia and Princess Luna
were mad at each other.
Now they are friends again.

Sometimes families live together
or get together for parties...

...like the Apple family.

And sometimes the ponies and friends
who live together become a family,
like Twilight and Spike.

Fluttershy has lots of pets.

She treats them like family.

They love Fluttershy very much.

Opalescence is Rarity's cat.

She is part of her family.

Pinkie lives with the Cake family.

She works with them in their bakery.

They help one another like family.

Sports teams are another
kind of family.
The Wonderbolts train
together every day.

Best friends are also like a family.
The Cutie Mark Crusaders are
like sisters.

Twilight, Applejack, Fluttershy, Rarity, Pinkie, Rainbow Dash, and Spike are close friends and make up a special family.

No matter where a pony lives,
they are with their family
when they feel love.

The Gift of Maud Pie

adapted by **Jennifer Fox**
based on the episode **"The Gift of Maud Pie"**
written by **Michael P. Fox & Wil Fox**

LITTLE, BROWN AND COMPANY
New York Boston

**Attention, My Little Pony fans!
Look for these words when you read this book.
Can you spot them all?**

present

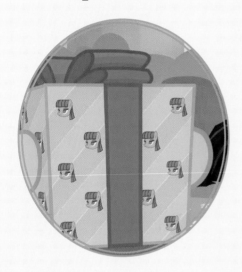

menu

sign

cannon

Pinkie Pie is so excited.

It is Pie Sister Secret Swap Day!

Today, she and her sister Maud will
spend the day together in Manehattan.
Then they will give each other presents.

Rarity joins Pinkie Pie and
Maud on their trip.
She has to find the perfect
spot for her new store.

Pinkie Pie has to find
something perfect, too.
She needs a present for Maud.

Pinkie and Rarity make a secret plan
so Pinkie Pie can buy a present.
"I will have fun with Maud at lunch,"
Rarity says.

"And I will go buy a pouch for her pet rock, Boulder," Pinkie says.

"Maud will LOVE it!"

Exploring the city is so much fun!
Manehattan is full of things to see like
the Pony of Liberty and Rockafilly Center.

"Yay!" Pinkie shouts.

Soon, it is time for lunch
and the secret plan.

Rarity winks at Pinkie Pie.

"Look, Maud.

Here is a menu!" Rarity says.

"I am going to wash my hooves,"
Pinkie says.

Pinkie Pie races down the street.
She finds the rock pouch shop!

"Perfect," Pinkie says.

She pushes the door,
but nothing happens.

Then she sees a sign.
The store is closed!

Pinkie Pie is sad.

How will she get

Maud's rock pouch now?

She has to think fast.

It is almost time to swap presents.

Then Pinkie Pie sees something!

A pony on the street
has the same rock pouch
Pinkie wants to buy.
"Excuse me!" Pinkie calls
as she runs after him.

"I really, really, really
need that pouch," she begs.

"Maybe," the pony says.

"For the right price."

"Anything!" Pinkie says.

"I want your party cannon,"
the pony says.

Pinkie Pie loves her cannon,
but she loves Maud more.

She trades the cannon for the rock pouch.

Pinkie Pie rushes back
to meet Rarity and Maud.

"You are back!" Rarity cries.

"Your hooves must be sparkling.
You were away for a long time!"

Soon, Pinkie and Maud
swap presents.
Pinkie gives Maud the pouch.

"It is for Boulder!" she cries.

Maud gives Pinkie confetti
for her party cannon.
"Wait," says Maud.
"Where is your party cannon?"

Pinkie Pie tells Maud she traded her cannon for the rock pouch.

"Let's go," Maud says.

"Where?" asks Pinkie.

"To get your cannon," says Maud.

They find the pony
with Pinkie's cannon,
but he does not want
to trade back.

Maud gives him
a few angry looks.
He agrees to take
the trade.

Maud will do anything
for Pinkie Pie,
and Pinkie will do
anything for Maud.

That's what friends and sisters do.

Pinkie Pie Keeps a Secret

Adapted by **Magnolia Belle**
Based on the episode
"The One Where Pinkie Pie Knows"
written by **Gillian M. Berrow**

LITTLE, BROWN AND COMPANY
New York   Boston

Attention, My Little Pony fans!
Look for these words when you read this book. Can you spot them all?

cupcakes

disguise

snacks

certificate

Pinkie Pie is making cupcakes at Sugarcube Corner when Mrs. Cake gets a special letter.

The letter says Princess Cadance
and Shining Armor want a cake
for their brand-new baby!

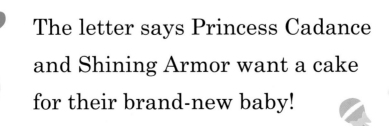

Mrs. Cake tells Pinkie Pie
that the new baby is a secret.
Pinkie Pie gulps.
"I have to keep a secret!"

Later, Pinkie Pie joins her friends
in Twilight Sparkle's castle.
The princess has news!

Twilight says that she is throwing a party for her big brother, Shining Armor, and Princess Cadance.

"And?" Pinkie Pie asks.

Twilight says that is all the news.

Pinkie Pie still has to keep the secret.

The friends decorate the castle
as a surprise for Shining Armor.
Talking about surprises makes
Pinkie Pie scared.
She is afraid she will tell the secret!

Twilight Sparkle finds a toy
that Shining Armor used to
play with as a baby.
Hearing the word "baby"
makes Pinkie Pie scared, too.

She asks the other ponies

if it is okay to tell a secret.

Rarity says no.

Pinkie Pie thinks she needs
to be alone to keep the secret.

Back at Sugarcube Corner,

Mr. Cake asks her to deliver orders.

Pinkie Pie is scared.

How will she keep the secret?

First, Pinkie Pie wears a disguise.
The Cutie Mark Crusaders can
tell it is their friend.
They ask if there is any news.
"Nope!" she says.

Next, Pinkie Pie sees Fluttershy.
She asks Pinkie Pie to bring snacks
like baby carrots to the party.
"Baby carrots?"
Pinkie Pie runs away.

Pinkie Pie decides the only way to keep a secret is to stay away from everypony.

Every time she sees another pony,

she zips by before they can say hello.

After she is done, Pinkie Pie is tired.
She still has to go to the party.

Pinkie Pie brings snacks
to the castle.
All the ponies are busy
getting ready.

Soon, Princess Cadance
and Shining Armor arrive
for the party!

Shining Armor has a game
for the ponies.
Twilight and her friends have
to find clues.
All the clues will reveal a surprise!

Shining Armor says that the first clue
is "where young ones spend their week."
The ponies think.

They find a clue in the schoolhouse!
It says to look at Applejack's birth
certificate.
Pinkie Pie dashes to the town hall.

The next clue says they need to "find a
place to buy comfy beds for little heads."
They need to find a baby crib!

The next clue tells them to "take a break where they can get a slice of cake."

The ponies go to Sugarcube Corner
and find Shining Armor and
Princess Cadance!
Princess Cadance tells Twilight to think
about what the clues have in common.

Twilight Sparkle looks at the clues: the schoolhouse, Applejack's birth certificate, a baby crib.

Twilight gasps!

Princess Cadance and Shining Armor
announce, "We are having a baby!"

Twilight Sparkle asks,
"I am going to be an aunt?
That is the best surprise ever!"

Pinkie Pie is so happy.

"I did it!

I kept the secret!" she cries.

Everypony celebrates the good news
with cake!
Princess Cadance thanks Pinkie Pie
for keeping the secret.
Pinkie Pie laughs.
"Aw, it was a piece of cake."

Meet Starlight Glimmer

written by **Magnolia Belle**

LITTLE, BROWN AND COMPANY
New York   Boston

Attention, My Little Pony fans!
Look for these words when you read this book. Can you spot them all?

cutie mark

mess

picnic

relax

Starlight Glimmer is a new
Unicorn in Ponyville.
She learns about magic from
Princess Twilight Sparkle.

Starlight Glimmer loves to learn.
She learns a lot about being
a good friend.

Starlight did not always
want to be a good friend.
She was not nice.

One time, she used magic
to give all ponies
the same cutie mark!

Another time, she tried to stop
Rainbow Dash's Sonic Rainboom.

Twilight saved the day!
She told Starlight about
the Magic of Friendship
and invited her to Ponyville.

Twilight helped Starlight
make new friends with Pinkie Pie,
Rainbow Dash, Fluttershy,
Applejack, and Rarity.

Starlight remembers her old friend Sunburst.
He moved to Canterlot to study magic.

Starlight gets to see Sunburst today!

She is excited, but she is also nervous.

Starlight and Sunburst are both shy.
They do not talk at first.

Starlight uses her magic
to help Sunburst.
They are not shy anymore!

Starlight and Sunburst are
good friends!

Twilight is proud of Starlight
for being a good friend to Sunburst.
Starlight wants to make more friends!

Starlight explores Ponyville
to find a new friend.

First, she bakes cakes
with Pinkie Pie and Mrs. Cake.
Her magic makes a mess.
Mrs. Cake is not happy.

Next, Starlight picks apples
with Applejack and Big Mac.
Her magic scares Big Mac.

Then Starlight visits Rarity.

They play dress-up.

Rarity says dressing up

is a good way to make friends.

Finally, Starlight has a picnic
with Fluttershy.

Starlight has a good day
but is sad she does not
meet new friends.

She visits Ponyville Spa to relax.

She needs to stop worrying.

At the spa,
Starlight meets Trixie.
She is nice!

Trixie once did mean things,
but she wants to be
a good friend now,
just like Starlight.

Starlight is so excited.
She tells Twilight
about her new friend.

Some ponies worry
about Starlight's new friend.
They do not know
Trixie is not mean anymore.

Starlight is a good friend to Trixie.
She says she is a good pony.

The new friends put on a great
magic show together.

Starlight Glimmer is happy
to have a new friend.
They really share the
Magic of Friendship!

We Are Unicorns!

by Jennifer Fox

L B

LITTLE, BROWN AND COMPANY
New York   Boston

Attention, My Little Pony fans!
Look for these words when you read this book.
Can you spot them all?

glow

potions

teacups

broom

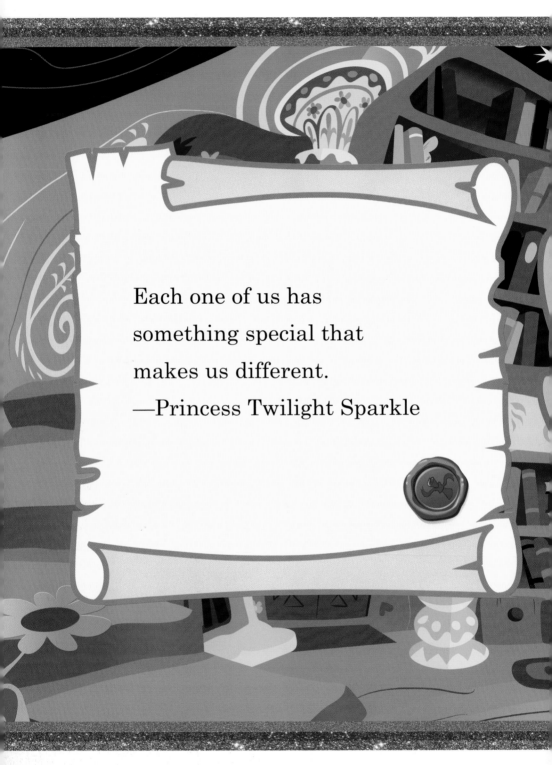

Each one of us has
something special that
makes us different.

—Princess Twilight Sparkle

Unicorns have a lot in common with their other pony pals.

Unicorns also have something
that makes them very special...

MAGIC!

Unicorns' horns glow when
they use their magic!

Tempest's horn is broken.

She has trouble with her magic.

Her horn shoots sparks!

Magic can make you shine brightly.

Magic can help keep you
safe and sound.

Magic can also help you find
a special new friend.

Even baby Unicorns have a
little bit of magic inside of them.

Magic is not always easy
for a Unicorn to control.

"Look out!"
Trixie brews up trouble
and turns everything into teacups!
Oops!

Keep trying, Sweetie Belle!
Make that broom zoom.

"It is working!"

Unicorns are full of magic—
and YOU are, too.

"Look for the magic inside of you!"

CHECKPOINTS IN THIS BOOK ✔

We Like Spike!

WORD COUNT	GUIDED READING LEVEL	NUMBER OF DOLCH SIGHT WORDS
140 ✓	G ✓	39 ✓

We Are Family

WORD COUNT	GUIDED READING LEVEL	NUMBER OF DOLCH SIGHT WORDS
358	K	59

The Gift of Maud Pie

WORD COUNT	GUIDED READING LEVEL	NUMBER OF DOLCH SIGHT WORDS
459	J ✓	74

Pinkie Pie Keeps a Secret

WORD COUNT	GUIDED READING LEVEL	NUMBER OF DOLCH SIGHT WORDS
556	K	85

Meet Starlight Glimmer

WORD COUNT	GUIDED READING LEVEL	NUMBER OF DOLCH SIGHT WORDS
360	K	59

We Are Unicorns!

WORD COUNT	GUIDED READING LEVEL	NUMBER OF DOLCH SIGHT WORDS
181	I	47